THIS LEVINSON BOOK
BELONGS TO:

_____

_____

for Hal, Flynn, Sean and Holly

I. W.

for Loki, Sorley and Finn

S. H.

First published in 1997 in Great Britain
by Levinson Books Ltd

10 9 8 7 6 5 4 3 2 1

Text © Ian Whybrow 1997
Illustrations © Sally Hobson 1997

A CIP record for this title is available from the British Library
The author and illustrator assert the moral right
to be identified as the author and illustrator of the work

ISBN 1 86233 082 4

Printed in Belgium

Parcel for Stanley

Written by
Ian Whybrow

Illustrated by
Sally Hobson

LEVINSON BOOKS

Everybody liked Stanley,
but nobody would ever –
just by looking at him –
think that he was clever.

Stanley ate his carrots.

He slept in his hutch.

But if you asked people, "What does Stanley do?"

People would say, "Not much."

His four best friends were always
busy busy busy.
They were a ginger cat, a duck, a fire engine
and a cow called Lizzie.

The cat was always climbing trees,
   the duck swam round and round;
the cow drove the fire engine
   and made the bee-bah sound.

Or if the fire engine got dirty
   and needed a wash,
the duck and the cat and the cow got some water –
   and they all went SLOSH!

They were worried about Stanley.
The cat said, "Meow.
Why don't you come and be busy with us?"
And Stanley said, "No thanks, not now."

He said he was expecting a parcel.

A parcel? Fancy that.

And when it came, do you know what was in it?

A book, a wand and a big top hat.

Next day, Lizzie saw stars shooting
  out of Stanley's ear.
She told the cat about it but the cat said,
  "Take no notice, dear."

That afternoon the queen phoned and asked to come to tea.

And the duck said, "Quack quack. We would be delighted, your majesty."

The friends were ever so excited.
They got some flags and flowers,
and they ran about and tidied up
for hours and hours and hours.

They told Stanley to keep out of the way,
because he was just a rabbit.
And they said, "Do stop waving that stick.
It's getting a bit of a habit."

At last the queen turned up for tea
  in her sparkly crown and shoes.
The cat and the cow and the duck took a bow,
  and Stanley and the fire engine said How-do-you-do's.

The queen said, "We would love to see
what all our subjects can do.
So come along and show us.
Duckie, let's start with you."

The duck said, "What can I do?
  Oh quack quack, let me see!"
And he gave the queen a lovely egg
  as green as green can be.

The cow said, "What can I do?
Oh moo, now let me see!"
And she gave the queen some lovely milk
to cool her cup of tea.

The fire engine said,
"What can I do?
Oh bee-bah, let me see!"
And he put up his ladder
and rescued the cat,
who was stuck
at the top of a tree.

And the cat went prrr-prrr for the queen
to show what cats can do.
And the queen said, "Now Stanley, your turn.
Please hurry, we're waiting for you."

And the others said, "Don't ask Stanley.
  Rabbits can't do much –
apart from eating carrots
  and mucking about in a hutch."

And at that moment
Stanley said,
"I'll *show* you. Just a mo."
And he waved his wand
And he disappeared . . .

Where's Stanley?

HEY-PRESTO!

And the queen said,
"Gosh, that's magic!
And frightfully clever, too!"

"Thank you," said Stanley, and bowed very low.
"Now you know what a rabbit can do!"

And then he did all the magic tricks
that he'd learned from his magic book.
For the wonderful thing about rabbits is –
They're much cleverer than they look!